This book belongs to:

. . . .

For Jake – best friend, best dog. A.S.
For Tegan, who really can. L.M.

OXFORD
UNIVERSITY PRESS

Great Clarendon Street, Oxford OX2 6DP

Oxford University Press is a department of the University of Oxford.
It furthers the University's objective of excellence in research, scholarship,
and education by publishing worldwide in

Oxford New York

Auckland Cape Town Dar es Salaam Hong Kong Karachi
Kuala Lumpur Madrid Melbourne Mexico City Nairobi
New Delhi Shanghai Taipei Toronto

With offices in
Argentina Austria Brazil Chile Czech Republic France Greece
Guatemala Hungary Italy Japan Poland Portugal Singapore
South Korea Switzerland Thailand Turkey Ukraine Vietnam

Text copyright © Amber Stewart 2008
Illustrations copyright © Layn Marlow 2008

British Library Cataloguing in Publication Data available

ISBN: 978-0-19-279248-8

10 9 8 7 6 5 4 3 2 1

Printed and bound by Imago in China

Amber Stewart & Layn Marlow

Little by Little

OXFORD

UNIVERSITY PRESS

Scramble was making a list.
A Can-do and a Can't-do list.

The Can-do side was much longer than
the Can't-do side. On it was:

forward roly-poly

backward roly-poly

being kind to frogs

mud sliding

making very
good sandcastles

slippery-rock
hopping.

The Can't-do side was
much shorter. It just said . . .

swimming.

'Whoever heard of an
otter who can't swim?'
asked Beaver.

'What? Not at all?' said Bear.
'Not even a little? At your age?
All your friends can swim.
Whatever next?'

'Obviously being kind to otters is not
on Bear and Beaver's Can-do list,'
Mummy said crossly, when Scramble told her.
'And I bet their sandcastles are rubbish,'
muttered Scramble's sister.

Sometimes, Scramble would pretend he could swim, but really he was hopping — very, very quickly — along the river bed.

Other times, he would run along the river bank, trying not to be left behind by his friends as they spun and tumbled through the water.

But most days, Scramble would simply sit on
his favourite slippery rock, wishing and wishing
— from his whiskers all the way down to his toes —
that he could swim.

Every day, his mummy
would say, 'Today's the day
you're going to crack it.'

And every day — it wasn't.

Then, one sunny Monday, Scramble and his sister were watching their friends jumping off the Highest-Ever Rock into the Deepest-Ever Pool below.

'You have got to start small,' his sister said.

'Small?' said Scramble.

'Yes, small,' she said. 'Come on, today really is the day to start small. Believe it, little brother, starting small turns can't-do into can-do.'

So, on that Monday, Scramble started small.
He hopped along the river bed, keeping his toes
off the bottom just that bit longer every time.

On Tuesday, he did higher hops
and floating (with holding on) in between.

On Wednesday, Scramble did floating with no holding on.

And, on Thursday, he did a little kicking
and then a lot of kicking to the Halfway Stone.

On Friday, Scramble splashed and kicked and swam the whole width of the river — from one bank to the other — all by himself.

And very soon (over Saturday and Sunday really),
that width became the length of the river from
Scramble's rock to the Deepest-Ever Pool.

Then the splashing and kicking turned
into gliding, and the roly-polies on the
river bank became underwater tumbling.

And, on Sunday evening,
as all his friends and family
gathered along the river bank
to cheer him on . . .

Scramble jumped off the
Highest-Ever Rock into
the Deepest-Ever Pool.

'I did it,' said Scramble to his sister.
'I can *really* swim!'

'You really can,' laughed his sister,
hugging her very wet little brother.

'You see. You started small . . .
and finished big!'